AF585398

TEXT TYPE
Procedure

The Body's Mighty Mini-Worlds

Systems in the Body

The body is made up of millions of cells. Cells are the smallest living things in nature. They are often called the building blocks of life. Cells form a number of mini-worlds in organisms.

The Nervous System

The nervous system includes the brain, our spinal cord and our nerves. It sends messages throughout the body.

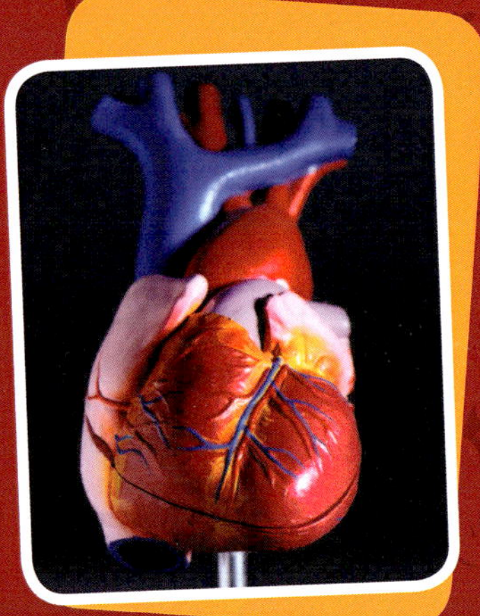

The Sensory System

The sensory system gives people information about the outside world. The eyes, nose, ears, tongue, skin and even the tiny hairs on the body all provide details of our surroundings.

The Circulatory System

The heart, arteries and veins are called the circulatory system, because they work together to circulate blood throughout the body.

The Immune System

The immune system is like a defence system. It helps to fight off viruses and bacteria that attack the body.

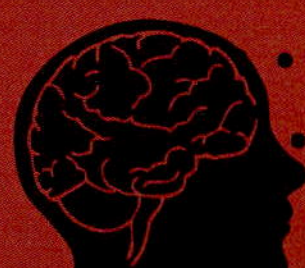

The Brain

My sincere thanks to the following people for their time, information, images and enthusiasm for this book:

Dr Tobias Merson and the team at the Florey Neuroscience Institutes, Melbourne, Australia.

Dear Reader

One day I had lunch with my neuroscientist friend. A neuroscientist is a brain scientist. I asked him why he loved studying the brain.

THE BRAIN IS LIKE THE PILOT OF A PLANE ... IT CONTROLS MANY MINI-WORLDS IN THE BODY.

He said that he was fascinated by the brain because it controls all that we do, think, say and feel. My friend's name is Doctor Tobias Merson and he is featured in Chapters 5 and 6 of this book. Find out how his research helps people with a disease called multiple sclerosis (MS).

I hope you enjoy reading about the mightiest mini-world in our bodies – the brain! I certainly enjoyed writing about this amazing topic.

Sharon Parsons

NELSON
CENGAGE Learning™
For learning solutions, visit **cengage.com.au**

Contents

The Brain

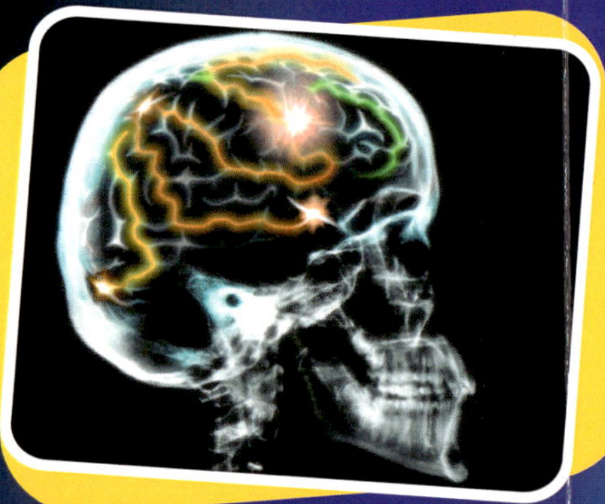

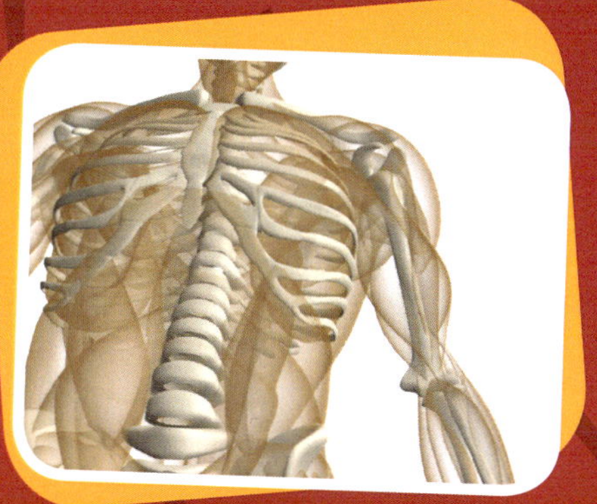

The Musculoskeletal System

The muscles and skeleton move the body. They also protect other organs.

The Digestive System

The digestive system is made up of the organs that get food in and out of the body: mouth, oesophagus, stomach, liver and other organs, some glands and the intestines.

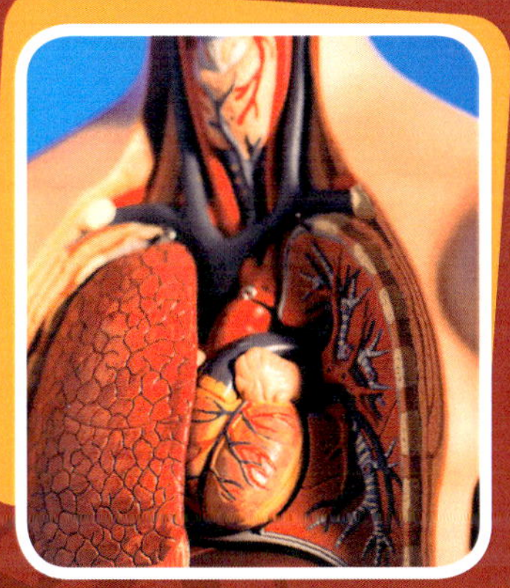

The Respiratory System

The respiratory system is made up of the organs that help us breathe, from the nose and mouth down to the lungs. This system works closely with the circulatory system to get oxygen to the cells.

Systems Need the Brain

The body's many systems need the brain to keep them all working together correctly. The brain is a very complicated organ – it is the mightiest mini-world in the body.

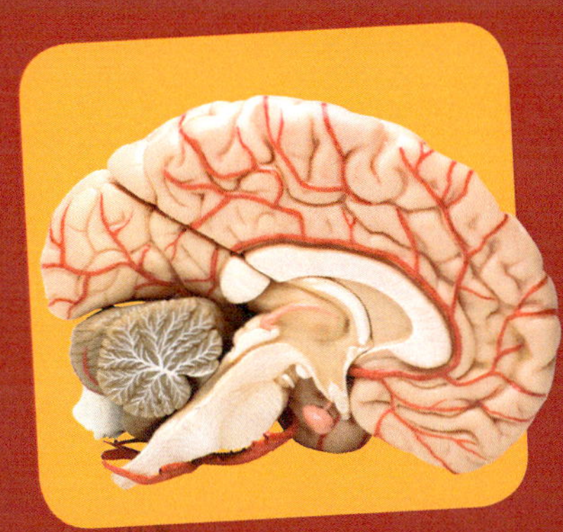

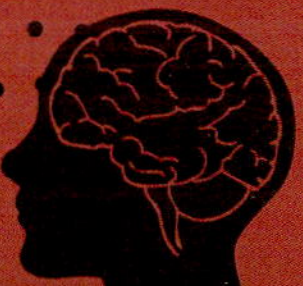

2 The Brain – the Mightiest Mini-World

The **Brain** Is in Control

Imagine that the body is like a plane. It contains many different systems to make it work. The body needs a "pilot" to keep those systems working properly. In the body, the brain is the pilot because it controls the systems.

The brain sends signals to the lungs and heart, so they keep working without us thinking about it.

The brain controls the senses, letting people see, hear, taste, touch and smell.

The brain releases chemicals into the body that make people feel different emotions, such as fear or joy.

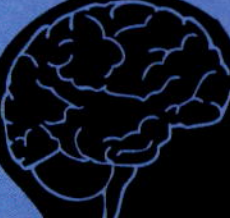

The brain controls movement, such as walking, running and playing.

The brain stores memories, which help people to recognise familiar people, places and things.

The brain allows people to think, reason, solve problems, and to talk about them, too.

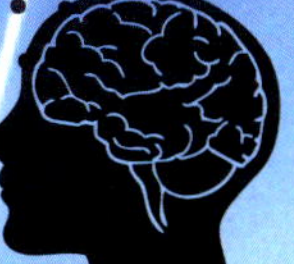

3 How to Have a Healthy Brain

brain food

Tips for a **Healthy** Brain

Because the brain controls the body, it is important to ensure that it can operate at its best. There are a number of ways to look after the brain.

Exercise keeps brains healthy.

Healthy Brain Tip 1

DO LOTS OF PHYSICAL ACTIVITIES

Physical activities, such as walking, running, swimming or climbing, bring oxygen to the brain. When we are active, the brain releases chemicals that make us feel good.

Healthy Brain Tip 2

DO LOTS OF MENTAL ACTIVITIES

Mental activities, such as problem-solving, learning new information, doing puzzles, playing games and reading books, keep your brain active.

Using the brain, especially in the first ten years of life, helps its development. If parts of the brain are not used, they stop developing.

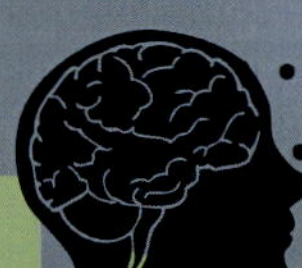

Healthy Brain Tip 3

EAT HEALTHY FOOD

Brains need fuel, too. The brain uses more energy than any other part of the body.

To give the brain energy and to supply it with the right balance of nutrients, eat lots of raw and cooked fruit and vegetables, protein (e.g. meat, fish, beans) and carbohydrates (e.g. bread, potatoes, pasta, rice).

Healthy Fish

Sardines have healthy oils.

Fish have a high amount of oils that contain omega-3 fatty acids. These are good for the brain. Fish with lots of omega-3 include salmon, sardines, ocean trout and tuna.

Healthy Brain Tip 4

DRINK LOTS OF WATER

The brain is about 80 per cent water. Water is vital for brain function. Drink lots of water, especially on hot days.

Water is essential.

Healthy Brain Tip 5

GET LOTS OF SLEEP

Brains need time to recharge at night. By getting at least eight to nine hours of sleep every night, the brain will be alert and recharged for the next day.

Sleep recharges your brain.

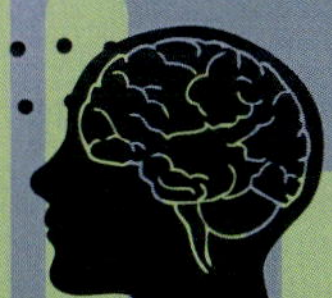

4 A Sleepy Brain Is a Good Brain

It's All About **Sleep**

To have a healthy brain you need a sleepy brain – but only at night! Most people need to have at least eight to nine hours of sleep every night. Sometimes younger people need more sleep.

"I'm going to bed!"

Getting enough sleep is a bit like charging a mobile phone. If you've used the phone a lot, you need to charge it for longer.

If you don't get enough sleep, you will not be able to:

- focus at school
- recall information easily
- think quickly while playing sports.

And you may feel extra grumpy!

Health

Jet Lag

If you travel from Australia to Italy, your body clock is set to Australian time. It wants to sleep during the Italian day and wake up during the night. This is called jet lag. Most people feel jet lag for the first days after a long trip, then their body adjusts.

"I'm really tired!"

Stages of Sleep

1

When the body is asleep, it goes through different sleep stages. One stage is called "rapid eye movement" (REM) sleep. During this stage, dreaming occurs, the eyes move and the muscles twitch.

2

All other stages are called non-REM sleep. One non-REM sleep is called "slow-wave sleep" (SWS). During this stage, the brain waves slow down and the body goes into a deep sleep.

3

Throughout the night, the body spends more time in non-REM sleep than in REM sleep.

Sleep Debt

Sleep debt is when you don't get as much sleep as you should. You can get very tired. Your brain is telling you that you "owe" it another hour or two.

Try to repay the sleep debt by going to bed earlier and getting more sleep the next night.

5 A Brain Scientist

Meet a **Neuroscientist**

A **neuroscientist** is a scientist who studies the brain to find ways to help people with brain illnesses. Doctor Tobias Merson is a neuroscientist who works at the Florey Neuroscience Institutes in Melbourne, Australia.

Neuroscientists do research to:

- understand what causes brain disorders
- discover new ways to stop, slow down or cure brain disorders
- develop new ways to help people better cope with brain disorders

When the brain does not work properly, it can make a person feel unwell. A brain illness can be very serious.

NEUROSCIENCE

Neuroscience: the science of the brain

Neuroscientist: a person who studies the brain

Neurosurgeon: a person who operates on people's brains

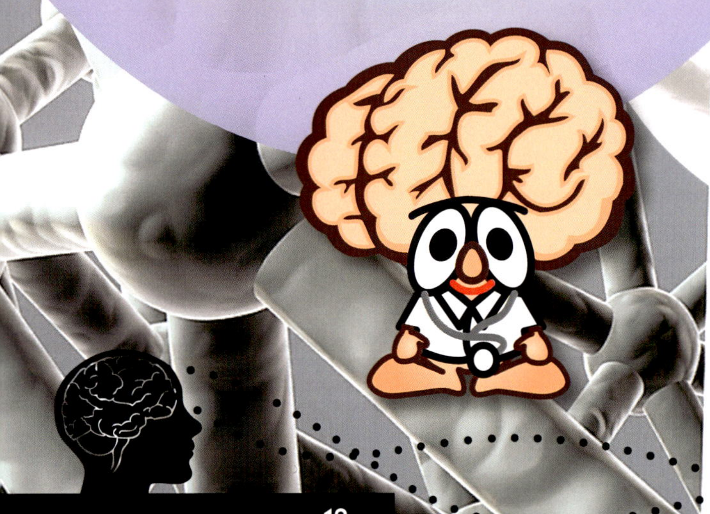

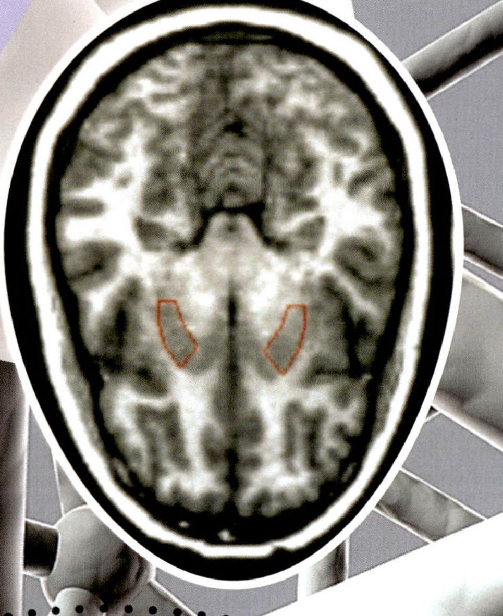

Social Studies

Who Was Howard Florey?

Howard Florey was a famous scientist who was born in Adelaide, South Australia. He led a team of scientists in England who found a way to use penicillin to help people to fight infections.

Penicillin has been used to help people with bacterial infections, such as bacterial meningitis, which can cause brain damage or death.

Howard Florey

Doctor Tobias Merson (far left) with his team at the Florey Neurosciences Institutes in Melbourne, Australia.

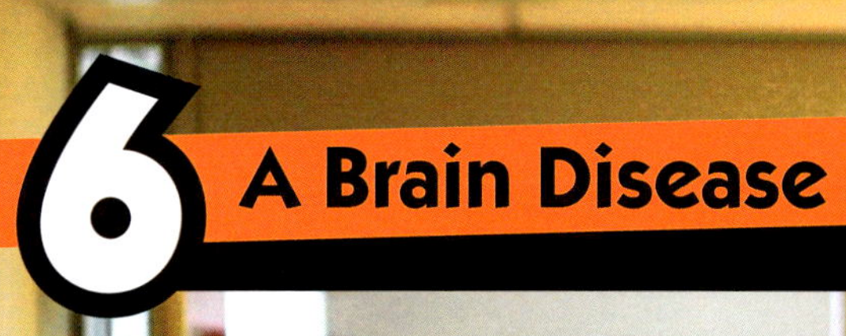

6 A Brain Disease

Multiple Sclerosis (MS)

One brain disease is called multiple sclerosis (or MS for short). For most people who have MS, the nerve cells in their brain find it hard to "talk" to the nerve cells in the **spinal cord**.

So when a person suffers from MS, they may have problems with:

- walking
- talking clearly
- seeing clearly.

They may also have many other health issues because of the disease.

SPINAL CORD

The spinal cord runs from the brain down the inside of the backbone to the nerves, to enable us to move, to feel, and to use our senses and our organs.

Neuroscientists Try to Find a Cure for MS

The neuroscientists at the Florey Neuroscience Institutes hope that their research will help to find a cure for MS.

Because the brain is so complicated, it can take years of research to learn about how a small part of the brain works.

More MS Facts

- Twice as many women as men have MS.
- MS is more common in colder climates than warmer climates.
- No one knows what causes MS.
- In Australia, about 20 000 people have MS.
- Around the world, about 2.5 million people have MS.

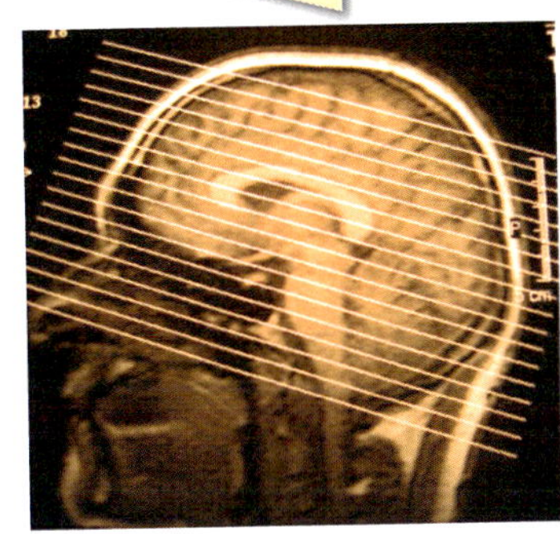

Brain illnesses can affect many people.

Dr Tobias Merson

Cost of Brain Research

It costs a lot of moncy to find cures for illnesses. The Australian Government funds part of the research for Dr Tobias Merson and his team at the Institute. Some people give donations to help pay for research into a cure for MS.

7 How the Memory Works

What are **Memories?**

Memories are information stored in the brain for a person to recall later. Memories may be:

- **Facts**: e.g. you may have learnt facts on an excursion that you need to remember for a class project
- **A Role in a Play**: e.g. you may have to remember your lines for a role in a school play
- **Movies or Books**: e.g. you might have seen movies, or read books that you want to share with your friends at school
- **Times and Dates**: e.g. important times and dates that your teachers or your parents have asked you to remember
- **Everyday Actions**: e.g. activities you have learnt how to do (like holding a pen, writing, understanding what words mean, and even turning the page of a book).

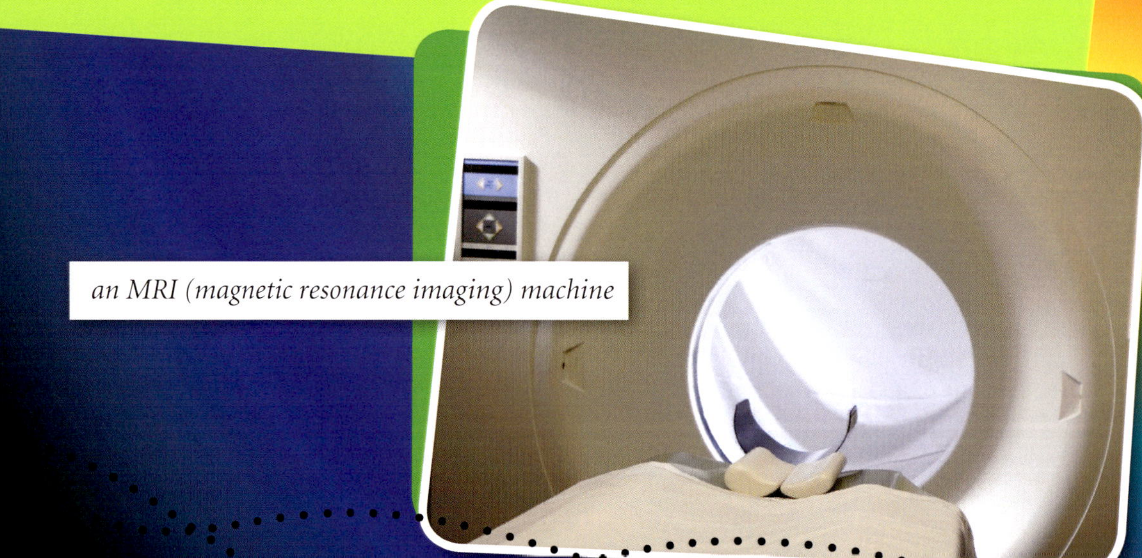

an MRI (magnetic resonance imaging) machine

A Memory Research Study

For years, scientists have researched how our brain remembers things. When doing research, all scientists follow a procedure. Pages 18–19 show a brief version of the procedure followed during some recent memory research.

The research topic was "How the Brain Makes a Memory".

The researchers were from the University of California, USA, and the University College London, UK.

a patient having an MRI

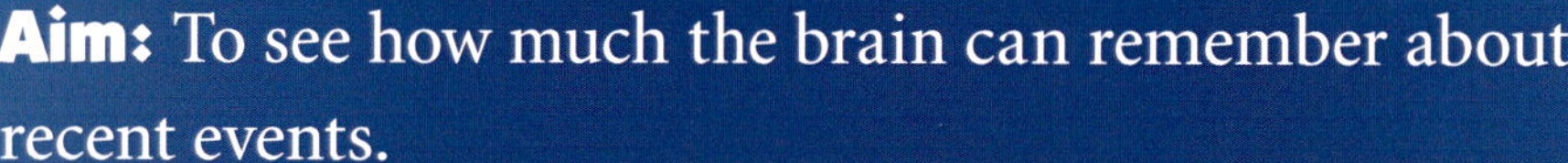

A **Procedure** for **Memory Research**

TEXT TYPE
Procedure

Aim: To see how much the brain can remember about recent events.

Equipment: computer display screens and a magnetic resonance imaging (MRI) machine.

Participants: people, or subjects, who volunteered to take part in the research.

Step 1

First, the subjects were asked to read words in different colours on different parts of the display screen.

Step 2

When the subjects read the words, the MRI machine scanned their brains. The MRI machine recorded how their brains were remembering the words.

Step 3

Next, the researchers wrote the words on word cards and added some new words.

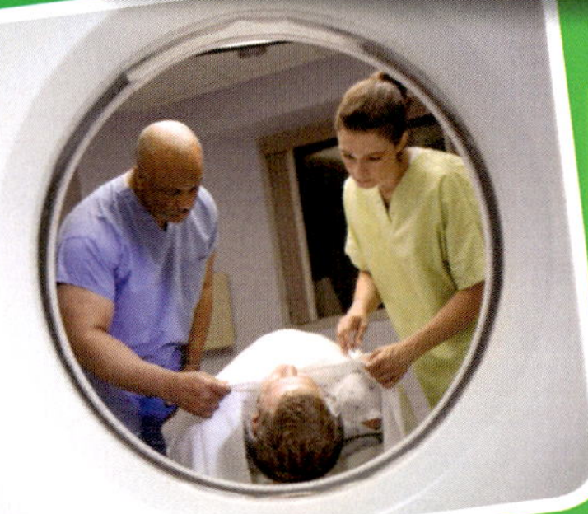

Step 4

Later in the day, the subjects were asked to read the word cards. They were asked to remember whether the word was from the display screen, or a new word.

Step 5

Finally, the subjects were asked to remember the colour and the location of the words on the display screen.

Conclusion

The researchers checked the MRI scans when the subjects were remembering the words.

The MRI scans showed an unexpected result. The subjects remembered both the colour and location of the words from the display screen.

The researchers thought that the subjects would only remember either the colour or the location.

The MRI scans showed that a part of the brain was working to help them remember both colour and location.

Try This Brain **Memory Research**

Aim: To test the brain's ability to remember words recently seen.
Materials: scissors; some blank paper, cut into 12 card shapes; one piece of A4-sized paper; five pens – red, green, orange, blue, black.
Participant: a friend to test in the research.

TEXT TYPE
Procedure

Step 1

Write four words in different colours on white cards:

- write "memory" in red
- write "brain" in green
- write "MRI" in orange
- write "researchers" in blue.

memory
brain
MRI
researchers

Step 2

Write these four new words in black pen on white cards: "recall", "colour", "location" and "screen".

recall
colour
location
screen

Step 3

Rewrite the coloured words from Step 1 as black words on white cards: "memory", "brain", "MRI" and "researchers".

memory
brain
MRI
researchers

Step 4

Draw a square for a computer display screen.

Step 5

Divide your square display screen shape into quarters.

Step 6

Place one coloured word card in each quarter of the square display screen.

brain	MRI
memory	researchers

Do Steps 7 to 12 of your research on the next page.

Step 7

Ask a friend to read each coloured word.

Step 8

Mix up the eight black word cards and put them on the table.

remember
colour
MRI
brain
location
memory
researchers
scree

Step 9

Ask your friend to read each word. Then ask which four words are new and which four words are from the square display screen.

Step 10

Mix up the four coloured word cards and put them on the table.

Step 11

Ask your friend to read the coloured words and tell you which quarter they were in on the square display screen.

brain
memory
researchers
MRI

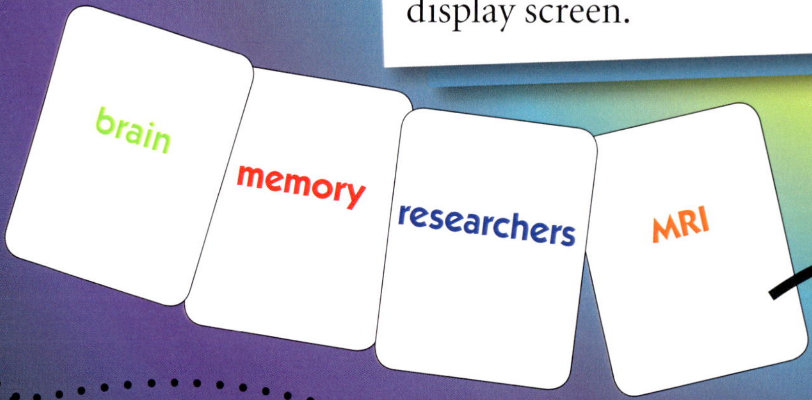

Conclusion

Write about the results of your research.

Q: In Step 9, how many words did your friend remember?

A: My friend remembered___new words and ___words from the square display screen.

In Step 9 my friend remembered	new words	words from the square display screen
	4	3

Q: In Step 11, how many times did your friend remember both the colour and the location on the square display screen?

A: My friend remembered both the colour and the location for ___words.

In Step 11 my friend remembered	words from both the colour and the location
	2

Social Studies

Brain Awareness Week

Every year for a week in March, people around the world do many activities in schools and communities to learn more about the brain.

Index

Glossary

arteries	Blood vessels that carry oxygen-rich blood being pumped away from the heart
bacteria	Micro-organisms that occur almost everywhere on Earth, some of which can cause illnesses
building blocks	The smallest units from which something (in this case, a body) is built
MRI scans	A process where digital pictures of the inside of a body can be made using powerful magnets
oesophagus	The tube that leads from the mouth to the stomach
omega-3 fatty acids	Natural fats that scientists believe may help protect people against some cancers, heart disease and brain illnesses
organs	Body parts that have a particular function, such as the brain, liver, kidneys, eyes and heart
veins	Blood vessels that carry blood low in oxygen into the heart